W9-BTT-400

With gratitude and respect I dedicate this special edition of The Fisherman & His Wife
to the people whose dream made the entire Once Upon A Time collection
a reality. Their unique vision continues to inspire me.

Tom Peterson   15 March 2001

Published in 2001 by Creative Editions
123 South Broad Street, Mankato, MN 56001 USA
Creative Editions is an imprint of The Creative Company
Designed by Rita Marshall

Printed in Italy
Library of Congress Cataloging-in-Publication Data
Von dem Fischer und seiner Frau. English
The fisherman and his wife / written by the brothers Grimm ; illustrated by John Howe.
Summary: The fisherman's greedy wife is never satisfied with the
wishes granted to them by an enchanted fish.
ISBN 1-56846-140-2
[1. Fairy tales. 2. Folklore—Germany. 3. Husband and wife—Folklore. 4. Fishes—Folklore.
5. Greed—Folklore.] I. Grimm, Jacob, 1785-1863. II. Grimm, Wilhelm, 1786-1859.
III. Howe, John, ill. IV. Title.
PZ8.V66 Fi 2001   398.2'0943'02—dc 21   [E]   00-067744

First Edition   5 4 3 2 1

The Fisherman & His Wife

Grimm

illustrated by John Howe

Creative Editions

Mankato

Once upon a time

THERE was a fisherman and his wife who lived together in a little hut close to the sea, and the fisherman used to go down every day to fish; and he would fish and fish. So he used to sit with his rod and gaze into the shining water; and he would gaze and gaze.

One day, the line was pulled deep under the water, and when he hauled it up he hauled a large flounder with it. The flounder said to him, "Listen, fisherman. I beg you to let me go; I am not a real flounder, I am an enchanted prince. What good will it do you to kill me? I shall not taste good. Put me back into the water and let me swim away."

"Well," said the man, "you need not make so much noise about it; I am sure I had better let a flounder that can talk swim away." With these words, he put him back into the shining water, and the flounder swam to the bottom, leaving a long, thin streak of blood behind. Then the

fisherman got up and went home to his wife in the hut.

"Husband," said his wife, "have you caught nothing today?"

"No," said the man. "I caught a flounder who said he was an enchanted prince, so I let him swim away."

"Did you wish nothing from him?" said his wife.

"No," said the man, "what should I have wished from him?"

"Well!" said the woman, "it's dreadful to have to live all one's life in a hut that is so small and dirty; you ought to have wished for a cottage. Go now and call him; say to him that we want a cottage, and he will certainly give it you."

"Alas!" said the man, "why should I go down there again?"

"Why," said his wife, "you caught him, and let him go, so he is sure to give you what you ask. Go quickly."

The man did not like going at all, but as his wife was not to be persuaded otherwise, he went down to the sea.

When he came to the sea it was quite green and yellow, and was no longer shining. So he stood on the shore and said:

"Once a prince,
But changed you be
Into a flounder in the sea.
Come! for my wife, Ilsebel,
Wishes what I dare not tell."

Then the flounder came swimming up and said, "Well, what does she want?"

"Alas!" said the man, "my wife says I ought to have kept you and wished something from you. She does not want to live any longer in a hut; she would like a cottage."

"Go home, then," said the flounder, "she has it."

So the man went home, and in place of the hut was a beautiful cottage, and his wife was sitting in front of the door on a bench. She took him by the hand and said to him, "Come inside, and see if this is not much better."

They went in, and inside the cottage was a tiny hall, a beautiful sitting room, a bedroom, and a kitchen and a dining room all furnished with the best of everything and fitted with every kind of tin and copper utensil. Outside was a little yard with chickens and ducks, and also a little garden with vegetables and fruit trees.

"See," said the wife, "isn't this nice?"

"Yes," answered her husband, "here we shall remain and live very happily."

"We will think about that," she said.

With these words they had their supper and went to bed.

All went well for a fortnight; then the wife said:

"Listen, husband, the cottage is much too small, and so is the yard and the garden; the flounder might just as well have given us a larger house. I would like to live in a great stone castle. Go down to the flounder, and tell him to give us a castle."

"Oh, wife!" said the fisherman, "the cottage is quite good enough; why would we choose to live in a castle?"

"Why?" said the wife. "You go ask; the flounder can quite well do that."

"No, wife," said the man, "the flounder gave us this cottage. I do not want to go to him again; he might be offended."

"Go," said his wife. "He can certainly give it to us, and ought to do so willingly. Go at once."

The fisherman's heart was very heavy, and he did not like going. He said to himself, "It is not right." Still, he went.

When he came to the sea, the water was all violet and dark blue, and dull and thick, and no longer green and yellow, but it was still smooth.

So he stood there and said:

"Once a prince,
But changed you be
Into a flounder in the sea.
Come! for my wife, Ilsebel,
Wishes what I dare not tell."

"What does she want now?" said the flounder.

"Ah!" said the fisherman, half ashamed, "she wants to live in a great stone castle."

"Go home, then; she is standing before the door," said the flounder.

The fisherman went home and thought he would find no castle. When he came near, however, there stood a great stone palace, and his wife was standing on the steps, about to enter. She took him by the hand and said, "Come inside."

Then he went with her, and inside the castle was a large hall with a marble floor, and there were dozens of servants who threw open the great doors, and the walls were covered with beautiful tapestries, and in the apartments were gilded chairs and tables, and crystal chandeliers hung from the ceiling, and all the rooms were beautifully carpeted. The best of food and drink was set before them when they wished to dine. And outside the house was a large courtyard with horse and cow stables and a carriage house—all fine

buildings; and a splendid garden with the most beautiful flowers and fruit, and in a park several miles long were deer and hares, and everything one could wish for.

"Now," said the wife, "isn't this beautiful?"

"Yes, indeed, said the fisherman. "Now we will live in this beautiful castle and be very happy."

"We will consider the matter," said his wife, and they went to bed.

The next morning the wife woke up first at daybreak, and looked from the bed at the beautiful country stretched before her. Her husband was still sleeping, so she dug her elbow into his side and said: "Husband, get up and look out the window. Could we not become king of all this land? Go down to the flounder and tell him we want to be king."

"Oh, wife!" replied her husband, "why should we be king? *I* don't want to be king."

"Well," said his wife, "if you don't want to be king, *I* will be king. Go down to the flounder; I will be king."

"Alas! wife," said the fisherman, "why do you want to be king? I can't ask him that."

"And why not?" said his wife. "Go down at once. I must be king."

So the fisherman went, though much vexed that his wife wanted to be king. "It is not right! It is not right," he thought. He did not wish to go, yet he went.

When he came to the sea, the water was a dark grey color, and it was heaving against the shore. So he stood and said:

"Once a prince,
But changed you be
Into a flounder in the sea.
Come! for my wife, Ilsebel,
Wishes what I dare not tell."

"What does she want now?" asked the flounder. "Alas!" said the fisherman, "she wants to be king."

"Go home, then; she is that already," said the flounder.

The fisherman went home, and when he came near the palace he saw that it had become much larger, and that it had great towers and splendid ornamental carving on it. A sentinel was standing before the gate, and there were numbers of soldiers with kettledrums and trumpets. When he went into the palace, he found that everything was of pure marble and gold, and the curtains of damask had tassels of gold.

Then the doors of the hall flew open, and there stood the whole court around his wife, who was sitting on a high throne of gold and diamonds. She wore a great golden crown and had a sceptre of gold and precious stones in her hand, and by her on either side stood six pages in a row, each one a head taller than the next. Then he went before her and said:

"Ah, wife! are you king now?"

"Yes," said his wife, "now I am king."

He stood looking at her, and when he had looked for some time, he said:

"Let that be enough, wife, now that you are king! Now we have nothing more to wish for."

"Nay, husband," said his wife restlessly, "my wishing powers are boundless; I cannot restrain them any longer. Go down to the flounder; king I am, now I must be emperor."

"Alas! wife," said the fisherman, "why do you want to be emperor?"

"Husband," she said, "go to the flounder; I *will* be emperor."

"Ah, wife," he said, "he cannot make you emperor; I don't want to ask him that. There is only one emperor in the kingdom. Indeed, he cannot make you emperor."

"What!" said his wife. "I am king, and you are my husband. You will go at once. Go! If he can make me a king he can make me an emperor, and emperor I must and will be. Go!"

So the fisherman had to go. But as he went, he felt quite frightened and thought to himself, "This can't be right; to be emperor is too ambitious; the flounder will certainly deny my request."

Thinking this he came to the shore. The sea was quite black and thick, and it was breaking high on the beach; the foam was flying about, and the wind was blowing; everything looked bleak. The fisherman was chilled with fear. He stood and said:

"Once a prince,
But changed you be
Into a flounder in the sea.
Come! for my wife, Ilsebel,
Wishes what I dare not tell."

"What does she want now?" asked the flounder.

"Alas! flounder," he said, "my wife wants to be emperor."

"Go home," said the flounder, "she is that already."

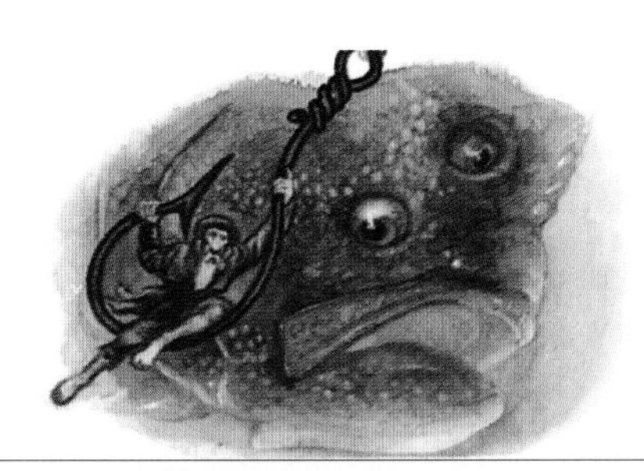

Then the fisherman went home, and when he arrived he saw the whole castle was made of polished marble, ornamented with alabaster statues and gold. Before the gate, soldiers were marching, blowing trumpets and beating drums. Inside the palace were barons, counts, and dukes acting as servants; they opened the door, which was made of beaten gold. And when he entered, he saw his wife upon a throne that was made of a single block of gold, and which was a full nine feet high. She had on a great golden crown which was likewise three yards high and set with brilliant and sparkling gems. In one hand she held a sceptre, and in the other the imperial globe. On either side of her stood two rows of armed soldiers, each smaller than the other, from a seven-foot giant to the tiniest dwarf no taller than my little finger. Many princes and dukes were standing before her. The fisherman went up to her quietly and said:

"Wife, are you emperor now?"

"Yes,"she said, "I am emperor."

He stood looking at her magnificence, and when he had watched her for some time, said:

"Oh, wife, let that be enough, now that you are emperor."

"Husband," she said, "why are you standing there? I am emperor now, and I want to be pope, too; go down to the flounder."

"Alas! wife," said the fisherman, "what more do you want? You cannot be pope; there is only one pope in Christendom, and the flounder cannot make you that."

"Husband," she said, "I will be pope. Go down quickly; I must be pope today."

"No, wife," said the fisherman, "I cannot ask him that. It is not right; it is too much. The flounder cannot make you pope."

"Husband, what nonsense!" she said. "If he can make me emperor, he can make me pope, too. Go down this instant; I am emperor and you are my husband. Be off at once!"

So he was frightened and went out; but he felt quite faint and trembled and shook, and his legs began to give way under him. The wind was blowing fiercely across the land, and the clouds flying across the sky looked as gloomy as if it were night; the leaves were being blown from the trees; the water was foaming and seething and dashing upon the shore, and in the distance the fisherman saw the ships in great distress, dancing and tossing on the waves. Still the sky was very blue in the middle, although at the sides it was an angry red as in a great storm. So he stood shuddering in anxiety, and said:

"Once a prince,
But changed you be
Into a flounder in the sea.
Come! for my wife, Ilsebel
Wishes what I dare not tell."

"Well, what does she want now?" asked the flounder.

"Alas!" said the fisherman, "she wants to be pope."

"Go home, then; she is that already," said the flounder.

Then he went home, and when he arrived there he saw, as it were, a large church surrounded by palaces. He pushed his way through the people. The interior was lit up with thousands and thousands of candles, and his wife was dressed in cloth of gold and was sitting on a much higher throne, and she wore three great golden crowns. Around her were a number of Church dignitaries, and on either side were standing two rows of candles, the largest of them as tall as a steeple, and the smallest as tiny as a Christmas tree candle. All the emperors and kings were on their knees before her, and were kissing her foot.

"Wife," said the fisherman, "are you pope now?"

"Yes," said she, "I am pope."

So he stood staring at her, and it was as if he were looking at the bright sun. When he had watched her for some time he said:

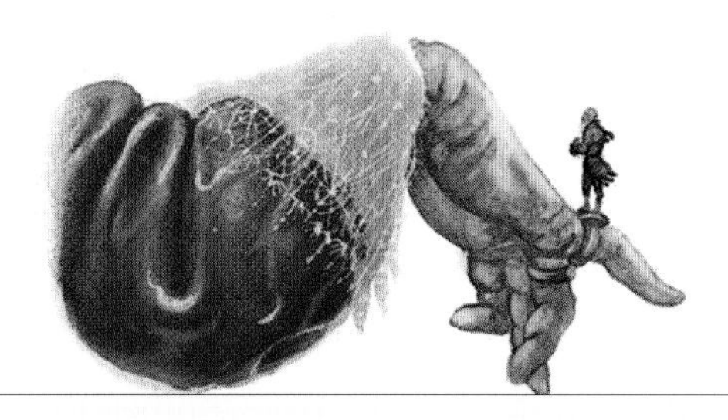

"Ah, wife, let it be enough now that you are pope."

But she sat as straight as a tree and did not move or bend the least bit. He said again:

"Wife, be content that you are pope. You cannot become anything more."

"We will think about that," she said.

With these words they went to bed. But the woman was not content. Her greed would not allow her to sleep, and she kept on thinking and thinking what she could still become. The fisherman slept well and soundly, for he had done a great deal that day, but his wife could not sleep at all. She turned from one side to the other the whole night long, and thought till she could think no longer, what more she could become. Then the sun began to rise, and when she saw the red dawn she went to the end of the bed and looked at it, and as she was watching the sun rise, she thought, "Ha! could I not make the sun and moon rise?"

"Husband," she said, poking him in the ribs with her elbow, "wake up. Go down to the flounder; I must be a god."

The fisherman was still half asleep, yet was so frightened that he fell out of bed. He thought he had not heard correctly, and opened his eyes wide and said:

"What did you say, wife?"

"Husband," she said, "if I cannot make the sun and moon rise when I appear, I cannot rest. I shall never have a peaceful moment till I can make the sun and moon rise."

He looked at her in horror, and a shudder ran over him.

"Go down at once," she said. "I must be a god."

"Alas! wife," said the fisherman, falling on his knees before her, "the flounder cannot do that. Emperor and pope he has made you. I implore you, be content and remain pope."

Then she flew into a rage, her hair flinging wildly about her face, and she pushed him with her foot and screamed:

"I am not contented, and I shall not be contented! You will go!"

So he quickly put on his clothes, and dashed madly from the palace.

But the storm was raging so fiercely that he could scarcely stand. Houses and trees were being blown down, the mountains were being shaken, and pieces of rock were rolling into the sea. The sky was as black as ink, it was thundering and lightning, and the sea was tossing in great waves as high as church towers and mountains, and each had a white crest of foam.

So he shouted, not able to hear his own voice:

"Once a prince,
But changed you be
Into a flounder in the sea
Come! for my wife, Ilsebel,
Wishes what I dare not tell."

"Well, what does she want now?" asked the flounder.

"Alas!" the fisherman said, "she wants to be a god."

"Go home, then; she is sitting again in the hut."

And there they are sitting to this day.